AF228578

Handling
Diabetes

by A. R. Carser

Content Consultant

Kyle J. Burghardt, PharmD
Associate Professor
Wayne State University

Handling
Health Challenges

Essential Library

An Imprint of Abdo Publishing
abdobooks.com

abdobooks.com

Published by Abdo Publishing, a division of ABDO, PO Box 398166, Minneapolis, Minnesota 55439. Copyright © 2022 by Abdo Consulting Group, Inc. International copyrights reserved in all countries. No part of this book may be reproduced in any form without written permission from the publisher. Essential Library™ is a trademark and logo of Abdo Publishing.

Printed in the United States of America, North Mankato, Minnesota.
052021
092021

Cover Photo: iStockphoto
Interior Photos: Shutterstock Images, 4, 26, 32, 38, 52, 64, 76; Larry St. Pierre/Shutterstock Images, 9; iStockphoto, 12–13, 19, 25, 34, 36–37, 44, 55, 60, 63, 73, 81, 85, 98–99; Wave Break Media/Shutterstock Images, 14; Charday Penn/iStockphoto, 20; Ronny Hartmann/picture-alliance/dpa/AP Images, 48–49; LightField Studios/Shutterstock Images, 68; Jemal Countess/Getty Images Entertainment/Getty Images, 86; Patrick Hertzog/AFP/Getty images, 92; FatCamera/iStockphoto, 96

Editor: Alyssa Krekelberg
Series Designer: Megan Ellis

Library of Congress Control Number: 2020948032

Publisher's Cataloging-in-Publication Data

Names: Carser, A. R., author.
Title: Handling diabetes / by A. R. Carser
Description: Minneapolis, Minnesota : Abdo Publishing, 2022 | Series: Handling health challenges | Includes online resources and index.
Identifiers: ISBN 9781532194979 (lib. bdg.) | ISBN 9781098215286 (ebook)
Subjects: LCSH: Diabetes--Juvenile literature. | Diabetes--Diagnosis--Juvenile literature. | Diabetes--Treatment--Juvenile literature. | Blood sugar--Juvenile literature. | Diabetes--Psychological aspects--Juvenile literature. | Health--Juvenile literature.
Classification: DDC 616.4/62--dc23

Contents

Chapter
One

Living with Diabetes

Chelsea felt a little dizzy as she and her teammates rode the bus to their basketball tournament. It was the first time the Little Bears, her team made up of all Anishinabe-Ojibwa girls, had qualified. *Time for a snack*, she thought to herself. Chelsea chomped on the apple and string cheese from her game bag as her teammates chatted excitedly around her. Her best friend, Monica, told Chelsea earlier that she had butterflies in her stomach so badly that she did not eat breakfast. Chelsea had replied that if she herself had done that, she would not be able to play in the tournament at all.

Chelsea had type 1 diabetes. She was diagnosed with the disease four years ago, when she was ten. Her mother and father had taken her to the doctor after she wet the bed. She had been so embarrassed.

People with diabetes have to make careful decisions about what they eat.

In the days before her accident, she had been very thirsty. It seemed like no amount of water could quench Chelsea's thirst. The doctors ran some tests on her blood and asked whether anyone in her family had type 1 diabetes. Chelsea's father mentioned that Chelsea's aunt did. In her follow-up visit to the doctor, Chelsea learned she did too.

For the last four years, Chelsea had used different medical devices to help her manage her diabetes. Her continuous glucose monitor had a tiny sensor inserted into the skin on her stomach. It measured the amount of sugar in her blood. When her blood sugar levels were high, the monitor told her insulin pump to deliver insulin, a vital hormone, to her pancreas. This helped bring her blood sugar to normal levels. She and her parents had to learn how to manually adjust the pump around mealtimes and anytime she felt dizzy, which is a sign of having low blood sugar.

Whenever she had a basketball game, Chelsea

did not wear her insulin pump or monitor. The physical contact during the game could harm her devices. On the day of the tournament, Chelsea tested her blood sugar manually and gave herself insulin injections. She had forgotten how easily she got dizzy when her blood sugar was low.

Fortunately, Chelsea's coach Melody was there to help. Melody had type 2 diabetes. She was diagnosed when she was 45 years old, after she noticed that everything she saw looked blurry. At the time, she also felt like she could never quench her thirst. Melody was a teacher and did not have a lot of time to exercise. She also felt she did not have the time or the money to make well-balanced meals. Melody's doctor diagnosed her with type 2 diabetes after testing her blood sugar and cholesterol levels and learning her sister, mother, and aunt also had type 2 diabetes. Melody's blood sugar levels were high. She had high cholesterol and blood pressure too.

After her diagnosis, Melody realized she had to make some life changes to help manage her disease. She and her sister got together three times a week to walk around their neighborhood for a half hour or more.

During the summer, Melody grew vegetables in her backyard garden. She also volunteered to coach the Little Bears. When she was a teenager, Melody loved to play basketball. Now, she could stay active while helping other young women fall in love with the sport too.

When Chelsea joined the team and told Melody she had diabetes, Melody was happy to support her. For the tournament, Melody brought extra healthy snacks. That way, she and Chelsea could manage their diabetes without sitting out for a single game.

Doctors recommend that people who have diabetes participate in sports or other forms of exercise to stay healthy.

What Is Diabetes?

Diabetes is a disease that affects the body's ability to use and store food as energy. There are two types. For people with type 1 diabetes, an organ called the pancreas produces little or no insulin. Insulin is a hormone that helps the body convert sugar into energy and store it for future use. For people with type 2 diabetes, the pancreas does make insulin. However, it may not produce enough, or the insulin does not convert sugar into energy as it should. In some cases, the pancreas may stop working altogether. It is common for people to be diagnosed with prediabetes, a condition where blood sugar levels are elevated, before being diagnosed with type 2 diabetes. Both types of diabetes can cause high levels of sugar in the blood. This condition is called hyperglycemia. When untreated, hyperglycemia can damage organs, nerves, and blood vessels.

Diabetes affects more than 34.2 million people across the United States.

"Diabetes affects 34 million people in the US, but its impact goes far beyond that. It affects everyone— family, friends, and loved ones."[3]

—American Diabetes Association

While most people with diabetes are adults, approximately 210,000 people who live with diabetes are under 20 years old. Diabetes affects people of all ethnicities. Approximately 14.7 percent of Native American adults live with diabetes, the highest percentage of any ethnic group in the United States. Approximately 12.5 percent of Hispanic adults live with diabetes, while 11.7 percent of Black adults do. Diabetes affects 9.2 percent of Asian Americans and 7.5 percent of white Americans.[4]

Diabetes among Native Americans

Native American adults are about twice as likely to be diagnosed with diabetes as white adults.[5] Family history, environment, and behavior all contribute to the number of people diagnosed with diabetes. Researchers also believe that the health of Native people today has been affected by harmful policies in the past. These include the United States' efforts to move Native communities off their historical lands and onto reservations, and to force children to attend government-run boarding schools away from their families.

Before these policies, the rate of diabetes among Native communities was very low. But living on reservations can make following many healthy traditions impossible. Today, most communities on reservations have unreliable access to fresh vegetables and fruits. They rely on convenience foods, such as sodas, chips, and other snack foods, which are high in carbohydrates and fat. These foods can lead to obesity, a risk factor for type 2 diabetes.

Diabetes is not curable, but it is treatable. Some people with type 2 diabetes can manage their disease with healthy diet and exercise alone. Others take oral medications that help them control their blood sugar. Many people with type 2 diabetes as well as type 1 diabetes use insulin pumps and continuous glucose monitors to help them manage their disease. Others use manual blood glucose tests and insulin shots. Millions of Americans attend school and work, raise families, perform music, and play sports while managing their diabetes. And since it is one of the most common diseases in the country, companies continue to work to create new treatments and technologies for diabetes.

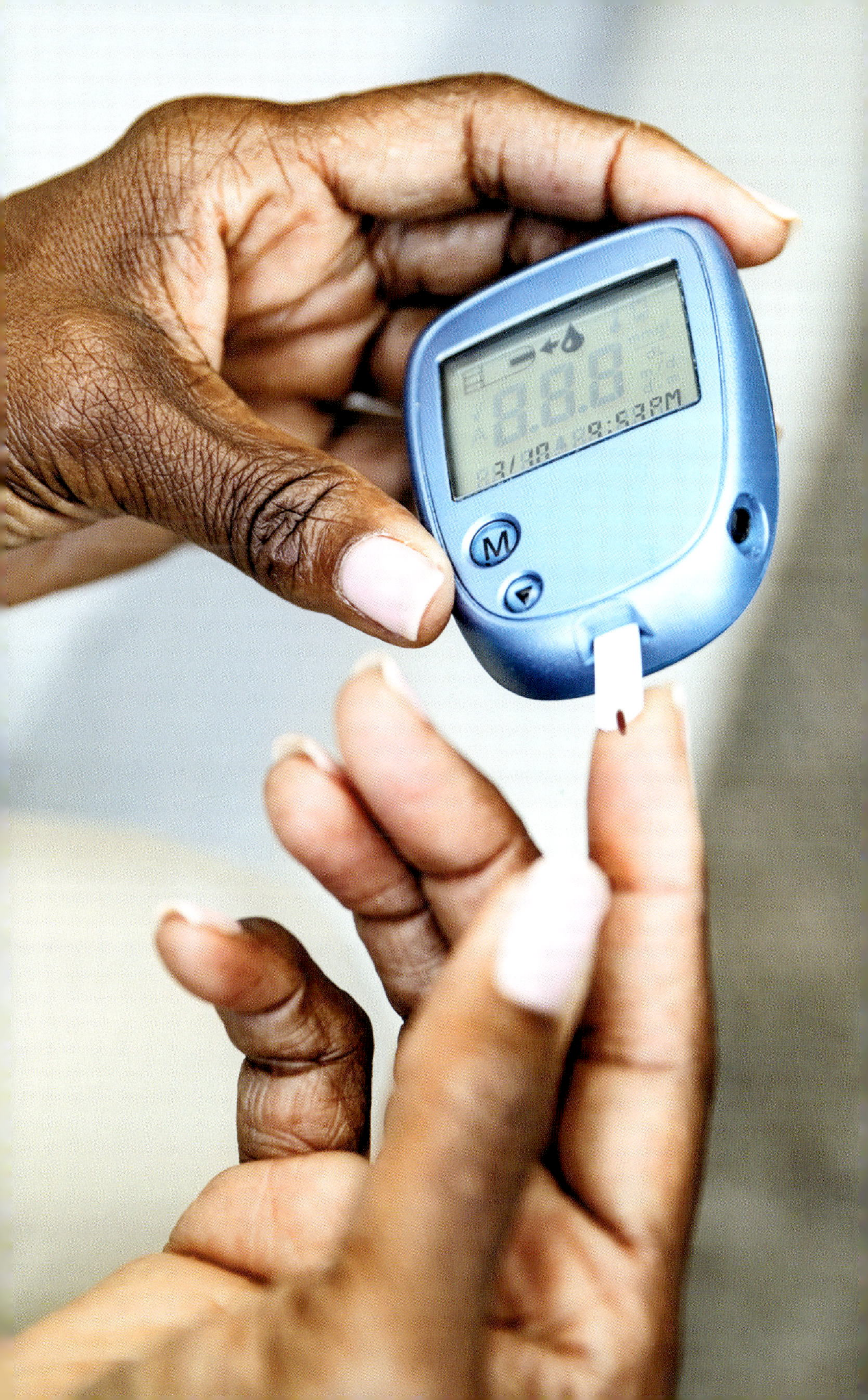

Chapter
Two

Type 1 Diabetes

Type 1 diabetes is an autoimmune disease. In this type of disease, the body's immune system attacks and destroys the body's own cells. In the case of type 1 diabetes, the immune system attacks specialized cells called beta cells. These cells are located in the pancreas and produce insulin. Over a number of months or years, the immune system destroys all of the body's beta cells. The body can make little or no insulin to convert sugar molecules into energy and store those molecules in the muscle and liver. Instead, the sugar molecules stay in the blood. This can cause hyperglycemia.

Medical researchers are still learning what causes type 1 diabetes. Often, people who are diagnosed with type 1 diabetes are related to someone who has the disease. However, this is not always the case.

Two symptoms of hyperglycemia are fatigue and headaches. Symptoms can develop over a few days or even weeks.

Some research has found that certain things in the environment may trigger the body's immune system to attack beta cells, leading to type 1 diabetes. One of these triggers may be a viral infection. If researchers can prove a connection, a viral vaccine may help prevent type 1 diabetes in the future. What researchers know for sure is that type 1 diabetes is different from type 2 diabetes and gestational diabetes, and that these two types of diabetes do not cause type 1 diabetes.

Type 1 and Vitamin D

Approximately 10 percent of people with diabetes have type 1 diabetes.[1] People of all ethnic backgrounds live with the disease. However, studies of type 1 diabetes demographics find more cases of the disease in people who live north of the equator. One possible explanation for the difference is exposure to sunlight. Sunlight helps the body produce vitamin D, an essential nutrient and hormone. People who live farther from the equator are exposed to less sunlight and may not get enough vitamin D. Some studies show that low vitamin D levels may be a risk factor for type 1 diabetes.

People of any age may be diagnosed with type 1 diabetes. However, most people are diagnosed with the disease in early elementary school or middle school. Physicians believe the hormonal changes during puberty may reveal the presence of the autoimmune disease.

The Honeymoon Phase

If diagnosed early enough, some people with type 1 diabetes experience what experts call a honeymoon phase. This phase may last a few months or a year. During the honeymoon phase, people may take some injected insulin. But they experience no symptoms of diabetes. Tests may show that the beta cells in the pancreas are producing enough insulin to manage blood sugar levels. However, the immune system is still attacking these beta cells. Eventually, most beta cells will no longer function. At this point, people will start to experience high blood sugar and other symptoms of type 1 diabetes. They will need to take insulin more frequently to manage their disease. The honeymoon phase will be over.

Getting Diagnosed

Before being diagnosed with type 1 diabetes, people living with the disease may experience several symptoms. Increased thirst and the need to urinate more frequently are common symptoms of type 1 diabetes. People with undiagnosed type 1 diabetes may also feel hungrier and eat more but unexpectedly lose weight. Dry mouth and itchy, dry skin are also symptoms of type 1 diabetes. When experienced together, these symptoms may prompt someone to make a doctor's appointment.

Before the appointment, the doctor may ask the patient not to eat for 12 hours before coming in. This is so the doctor can administer a fasting blood sugar test. This test measures the amount of sugar molecules present in the blood. In people without diabetes, a fasting blood sugar level of 99 milligrams per deciliter (mg/dL) or lower is typical. A fasting blood sugar level of 126 mg/dL or greater indicates someone has diabetes.

People use devices called lancets to prick through the skin and get blood for glucose testing.

In addition to the fasting blood sugar test, the doctor may also administer a glucose tolerance test. This test measures a patient's blood sugar levels before and after she drinks a sugary liquid. The first measurement is taken after a 12-hour fast. Then, the patient drinks a sugary liquid. The doctor measures her blood sugar levels after one hour and again after two hours. After two hours, if blood sugar levels are at 200 mg/dL or above, the patient likely has diabetes.

A person's blood test is sent to a lab for evaluation.

Two additional tests help doctors decide whether someone is suffering from type 1 or type 2 diabetes. Since type 1 diabetes is an autoimmune disease, someone with type 1 diabetes will have autoantibodies in his blood. These substances are produced when the body attacks itself. They will be present in someone who has type 1 diabetes, but not in a person with type 2 diabetes. The doctor may also test the patient's urine for ketones. These are chemicals the body produces when it is burning fat for energy rather than sugar. This is an indication of type 1 diabetes.

To make a type 1 diabetes diagnosis, a doctor will look at the results of these four tests. If someone has a fasting blood sugar of 126 mg/dL or greater, a glucose tolerance of 200 mg/dL or greater, and has autoantibodies in his blood and ketones in his urine, he has type 1 diabetes.

Treating Type 1 Diabetes

Once people are diagnosed with type 1 diabetes, they will work with their doctors to create management plans. While there is no cure for type 1 diabetes, the disease can be managed. People will have to test their blood sugar levels regularly throughout the day. Some people choose to take these levels with manual blood glucose tests. Others use continuous glucose monitors.

Since their bodies do not produce insulin, people with type 1 diabetes take medication to provide it. Many people with type 1 diabetes use insulin pumps to automatically provide a baseline level of insulin to the body. Others give themselves insulin injections.

Regular blood glucose monitoring and insulin injections are essential to managing type 1 diabetes. But diet, exercise, and controlling blood pressure and cholesterol are important parts of a diabetes management care plan too. People living with type 1

Type 1 Diabetes Devices

People living with type 1 diabetes use two key devices to manage their disease. A continuous blood glucose monitor is a sensor that is placed under the skin. It allows people to monitor their blood sugar levels instantly and over a period of time. If blood sugar levels get too high or too low, the monitor sounds an alarm.

An insulin pump is another diabetes management device. It is attached to the body through tubing or is attached directly to the skin. The pump has a short, thin tube called a cannula that is inserted under the skin. Through it, the pump delivers insulin into a layer of fatty tissue to be used by the body. Pumps release insulin the same way the pancreas would if it were functioning properly. A pump will release a small, continuous dose of insulin throughout the day. Before meals, the pump will release a larger dose of insulin. Many people wear their pumps all the time. Others will take a break from wearing their pumps for vacations or over the summer. If they do not wear pumps, people living with type 1 diabetes must give themselves injections of insulin.

diabetes work with nutritionists to identify healthy foods that will not cause spikes in blood sugar levels. They exercise regularly and make sure to get enough sleep. Most people with type 1 diabetes also visit their primary care doctors regularly to monitor their blood pressure and cholesterol levels.

Knowing that a person can manage his or her condition can feel empowering. Singer Nick Jonas has type 1 diabetes and said this about his disease: "Diabetes sounds like you're going to die when you hear it. I was immediately frightened. But once I got a better idea of what it was and that it was something I could manage myself, I was comforted."[3]

Complications and Risks

People living with type 1 diabetes can develop complications over time. These complications can be manageable, but they can also become disabling or life-threatening. Sometimes, people struggle to manage their blood sugar levels. Chronic high blood sugar levels can lead to other conditions, such as heart disease, kidney disease, and stroke. Some people with type 1 diabetes may experience eye problems, including blindness.

Others may experience nerve damage or poor blood flow in their feet and lower legs. If these areas are cut or develop blisters, these small wounds can create serious infections. In some cases, the infections become severe enough to require the amputation of a toe, foot, or leg.

When people with type 1 diabetes are unable to manage their diabetes, they may develop a life-threatening condition called diabetic ketoacidosis. This happens when the cells start to break down fat for energy because they are unable to access the sugar in the blood. This process creates toxic acids called ketones. A buildup of ketones in the body can cause weakness, vomiting, stomach pain, and fever.

People with type 1 diabetes avoid or reduce the effects of these complications by visiting their doctors regularly, watching what they eat, exercising, and taking their medications. People may see their primary care physicians to manage their diabetes and eye doctors and podiatrists to manage their eye and foot conditions. Working with a nutritionist is often helpful for people who struggle with high blood sugar levels. Type 1 diabetes may not be curable, but with the help of physicians and healthy choices, people with type 1 diabetes can live full lives.

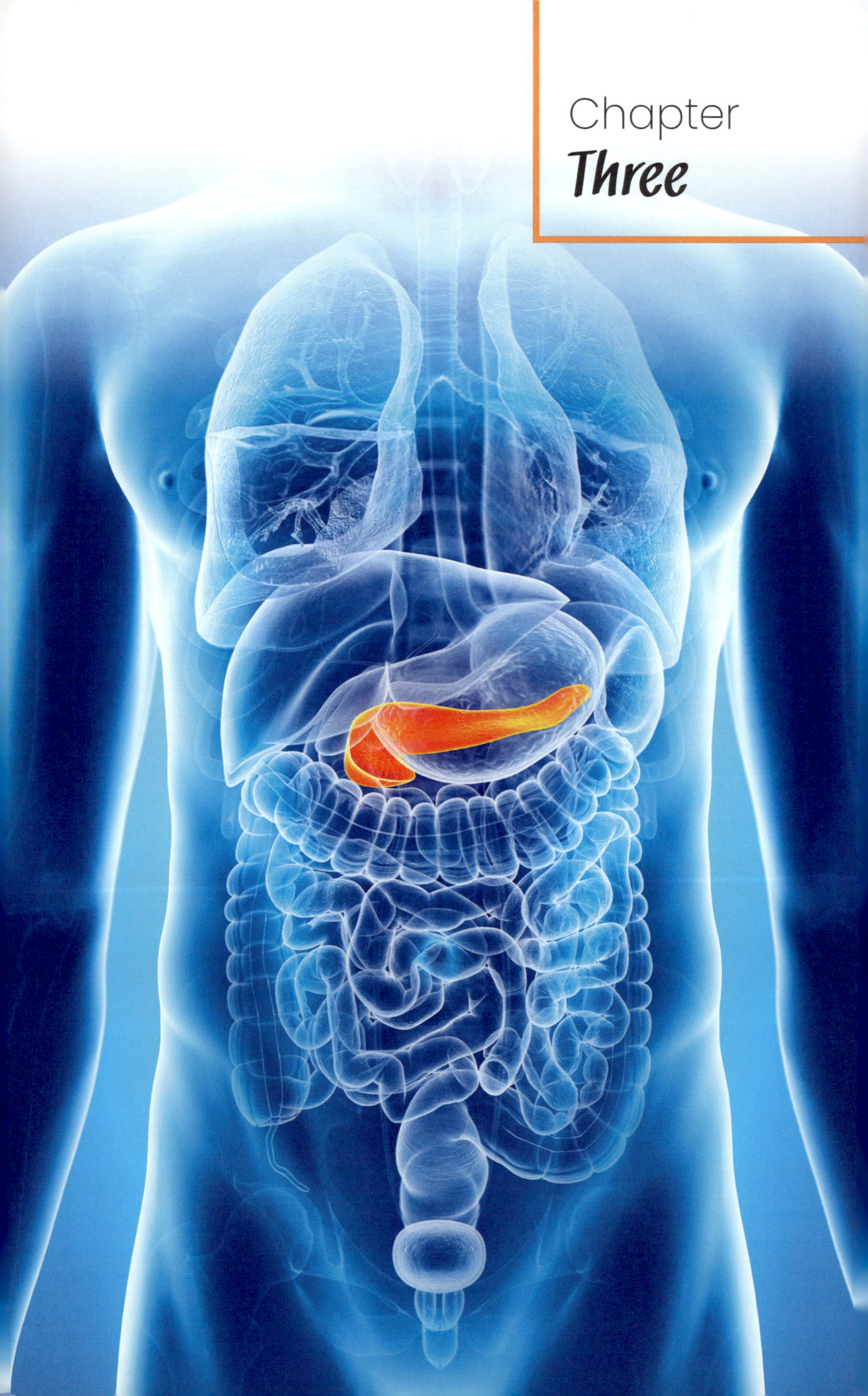
Chapter
Three

Type 2 Diabetes

Type 2 diabetes is far more common in the United States than type 1 diabetes. Approximately 90 percent of people diagnosed with diabetes are diagnosed with type 2 diabetes.[1] Type 2 diabetes is not an autoimmune disease, as type 1 diabetes is. Someone with type 2 diabetes has a pancreas that creates insulin. In some cases, the pancreas does not produce enough insulin for the body to properly control its blood sugar levels. In other cases, the body is unable to use the insulin it produces to help cells absorb glucose to use for energy. This is called insulin resistance.

The pancreas is behind the stomach and is approximately 6 inches (15 cm) long.

Causes of Type 2 Diabetes

Researchers do not know why type 2 diabetes develops. However, there are several well-known risk factors for acquiring type 2 diabetes. If someone's sibling or parent has type 2 diabetes, then she is more likely to develop it. Research has found that people who do not exercise regularly and are overweight or obese are also at risk for acquiring type 2 diabetes. Being physically active helps the body use glucose as energy. Fatty tissue can cause cells to become resistant to insulin.

Type 2 diabetes primarily affects adults, who tend to be less physically active than children. It is more difficult for adults to maintain muscle. But studies have found an increase in children and young adults being diagnosed with type 2 diabetes. This increase is related to the rise in obesity among younger Americans.

In the United States, people of color are more likely to be diagnosed with type 2 diabetes than white people. These include Native Americans, Latinos, Black people, and Asian Americans. The reasons for the difference are complex. Family history and lifestyle play a role. But so do other factors. Some people of color live in areas with little access to affordable healthy foods. These can include rural and urban areas where grocery stores are very far away. Latinos and Black people are less likely than white people to have health insurance, which can make trips to the doctor unaffordable or impossible. When treated, people of color tend to receive lower-quality care than their white counterparts too. All of these factors contribute to higher rates of type 2 diabetes in people of color.

Getting Diagnosed

The symptoms of type 2 diabetes are similar to those of type 1 diabetes. However, symptoms of type 2 diabetes tend to occur more gradually. People with undiagnosed type 2 diabetes may feel thirstier and hungrier than usual. They may feel irritable and tired more often. They may realize they are unable to see as clearly as they once did. Additionally, people with undiagnosed type 2 diabetes may find that they get skin or gum infections more frequently. These infections take longer to clear up.

Once someone has noticed these symptoms, it is time to see a doctor. The doctor will ask about family history of diabetes and about the patient's lifestyle habits. In addition to the fasting blood sugar test and glucose tolerance test, the doctor may perform an A1C test. The A1C test is a blood test that looks at a patient's average blood sugar level over the past two or three months. It measures the amount of glucose attached to hemoglobin. Hemoglobin is a protein found in red blood cells. If more than 6.5 percent of hemoglobin in the red blood cells have glucose attached to them, a patient has diabetes.[5]

To make a type 2 diabetes diagnosis, a doctor will look at the patient's A1C. She will also review the patient's fasting blood sugar and glucose tolerance tests. If these tests show higher-than-normal blood sugar levels, the doctor will diagnose the patient with type 2 diabetes.

Treating Type 2 Diabetes

Like type 1 diabetes, there is no cure for type 2 diabetes. Someone diagnosed with type 2 diabetes will work

Swimming works the whole body and is a great way to exercise.

Help with Type 2 Diabetes

Most people with type 2 diabetes are able to manage their disease independently with the help of doctors and family members. But friends can be supportive too. Lean protein, whole grains, and fruits and vegetables are healthy choices for everyone, and friends of people with diabetes can enjoy these foods as well. Friends can also offer to bike, kick a soccer ball, or shoot baskets on a regular basis with a friend who has diabetes. They should also know the signs of hypoglycemia and ask how to help in the event that the friend experiences the condition.

with his or her doctor to develop a management plan. Eating a healthy diet, exercising, and monitoring and managing blood sugar levels are essential parts of the plan.

Healthy diet and exercise can help many people with type 2 diabetes manage their disease. Healthy meals are full of lean protein, vegetables, whole grains, and fruit. People living with type 2 diabetes can enjoy sugary foods every once in a while. Thirty minutes of walking, running, swimming, or biking every day helps the body use up glucose and keep blood sugar levels low.

Some people living with type 2 diabetes use devices such as continuous blood glucose meters and insulin pumps to manage their diabetes. Others use manual monitors and insulin injections or oral medicines. Depending on the management plan, someone with type 2 diabetes may test his or her blood sugar levels up to four times a day or more.

While some people with type 2 diabetes can control their blood sugar levels by simply eating healthily, most people must use medications to control their disease. Some people with type 2 diabetes take medicines to help their bodies produce and use insulin. Some medicines help the pancreas make more insulin. Other medicines help tissues become more sensitive to insulin.

If the disease has progressed, it is common for people with type 2 diabetes to give themselves insulin injections throughout the day. They may use a needle and syringe, or they might use a device

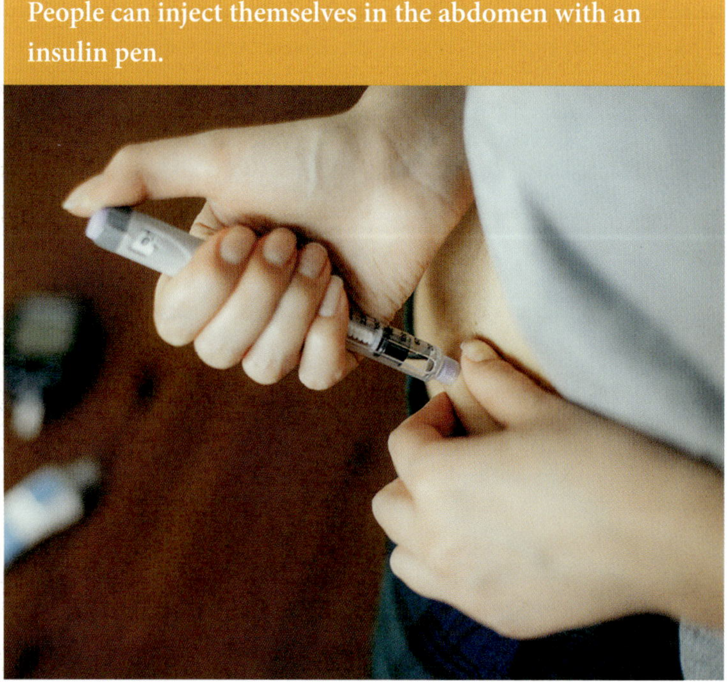

People can inject themselves in the abdomen with an insulin pen.

called an insulin pen.
Insulin is available in several
different types, including
rapid-acting doses that work
right away and long-acting
doses that provide insulin
over time. Many people use
a combination of insulin
types to manage their type 2
diabetes throughout the day.

Complications and Risks

The complications and
risks for type 2 diabetes are
similar to those for type 1
diabetes. People living with
type 2 diabetes have an
increased risk of developing
heart disease and kidney
damage. They may experience nerve damage in
their feet that can lead to infections, and in some
cases, amputations.

People living with type 2 diabetes may experience
hyperglycemia and its counterpart, hypoglycemia.
Hypoglycemia occurs when blood sugar levels

are too low. On the other end of the spectrum, some people with type 2 diabetes experience a life-threatening condition called hyperglycemia hyperosmolar nonketotic syndrome. This condition occurs when blood sugar levels are very high, over 600 mg/dL. Symptoms of the syndrome include dry mouth, extreme thirst, fever, confusion, and hallucinations. Often, people have been ill before the onset of this syndrome.

As with type 1 diabetes, people can avoid or minimize these complications by following their management plans and seeing their doctors regularly. People living with type 2 diabetes try to keep their blood pressure and cholesterol levels within healthy ranges. There is no cure for type 2 diabetes. But by following their management plans, people can live good lives with the disease.

Chapter
Four

An Ancient Disease

Diabetes is a disease that has affected people for thousands of years. From natural remedies to the discovery of insulin and other life-saving medications, medical experts have made great strides in the treatment of this disease.

Ancient Observations

The first known mention of the disease that would later be called diabetes occurred around 1550 BCE in ancient Egypt. Medical texts called the Ebers papyrus describe a treatment for excessive urination. This is a primary symptom of diabetes. The treatment called for a mixture of water, elderberry, and other natural substances.

In the 500s BCE, doctors in India were also studying the condition. They called it *madhumeha*,

The French lilac was once used to treat frequent urination, which is one symptom of diabetes.

or "sweet urine."[1] They observed that the urine of people with the condition attracted ants, just as honey did.

The ancient Greeks also observed and studied the symptoms of diabetes. In the 100s CE, Aretaeus of Cappadocia gave the condition its current name, *diabetes*, which means "siphon" in Greek.[2] A siphon is a device that moves water from a high place to a lower one. Aretaeus observed that people with diabetes seemed unable to absorb the liquid they ingested, as they released large amounts of urine. In the 400s CE, Sushruta, an Indian physician, and Charaka, a surgeon, identified the difference between the two types of diabetes.

Medieval physicians were also curious about the cause and treatment of diabetes. Persian physician Avicenna wrote about the disease in

1025 CE. He observed that the urine of people with diabetes smelled and tasted sweet. He also noted that people with diabetes had a condition called diabetic gangrene. Gangrene is a condition where tissue dies off due to infection or lack of blood flow. It typically affects the toes, fingers, and feet. To treat the condition, Avicenna recommended a mixture of lupin, fenugreek, and zedoary seeds. Meanwhile, people across Europe treated diabetes with French lilac.

Modern Science Rediscovers Diabetes

The methods doctors used to diagnose and treat diabetes changed little between the 1000s and 1600s. In 1674, British physician Thomas Willis conducted experiments on the urine and blood of people with diabetes. He found evidence of sugar in both their urine and blood. His findings were confirmed 102 years later by Matthew Dobson. Dobson took the urine from a person with diabetes and dried it out. What remained was a white, granular substance that looked, smelled, and tasted like sugar.

Physicians continued to study diabetes in the 1800s. French doctor Claude Bernard studied the liver and its connection to diabetes. In 1857, he discovered the liver produced a substance that affected blood sugar levels. This substance was glycogen, which is glucose in its stored form.

In 1869, German doctoral student Paul Langerhans, just 22 years old, described the existence of special cells in the pancreas that he called pancreatic islets. These are the beta cells in the pancreas that produce insulin.

In 1899, German doctors Oskar Minkowski and Joseph von Mering discovered the role of the pancreas. They removed the pancreases of dogs and observed what happened. The dogs whose pancreases were removed developed diabetes and died. With this experiment, Minkowski and von Mering proved the essential function of the pancreas.

In the United States, physicians researched the effects of diet and exercise on the treatment of diabetes. Elliott Joslin and Frederick Allen took an aggressive approach to treating diabetes, recommending that people tightly control the amount of food they ate. While this made patients chronically hungry, it did help them lower their blood sugar levels. Other physicians chose a different treatment. They understood restricting carbohydrates in particular helped control blood sugar levels. These physicians put their patients on a diet of primarily meat and vegetables. By reducing their carbohydrate intake, most patients were able to reduce their blood sugar levels. After 1921, most physicians also recommended patients add one more thing to their treatment regimen: insulin.

There are many healthy and delicious meals that people with diabetes can make.

Treatment in the 1900s

Until the 1900s, diabetes—especially type 1 diabetes—was considered a fatal disease. No medicines existed to treat it until the 1920s. Up to that time, people treated the symptoms of the disease with herbal remedies, special diets, and physical activity. People living with type 1 diabetes died decades earlier than people who did not suffer from the disease. People with type 2 diabetes also had shorter life spans.

In 1921, Canadian physicians Frederick Banting and Charles Best built upon the work of Langerhans, Minkowski, and von Mering. Banting and Best found a way to isolate insulin, the hormone that helps cells use glucose for energy. In 1926, American chemist John Jacob Abel purified insulin and was able to isolate it in its crystalline form. This discovery improved the purity of insulin.

In the 1950s, drug companies developed several oral medicines that helped people with diabetes manage their disease. Metformin was developed in 1959. It lowers blood sugar levels by reducing glucose

Frederick Banting and Charles Best

Frederick Banting was a surgeon during World War I (1914–1918). After the war, he returned to Canada to begin his medical research career at the University of Toronto. There, he collaborated with students, including Charles Best. Together, Banting and Best studied how the body metabolizes carbohydrates. Part of this work was learning about the function of the pancreas. The two men discovered that when they removed insulin from the pancreas, the blood sugar levels of their test animals spiked. They had discovered insulin and the role it plays in the body. In 1922, the two treated their first human patient, a 14-year-old boy with diabetes named Leonard Thompson. Banting and Best extracted insulin from the pancreas of a cow. Then, they injected this insulin into Leonard. Shortly after, Leonard's blood sugar levels dropped. In 1923, Banting won the Nobel Prize in Medicine for this work.

production and is still prescribed today. Tolbutamide is another drug that lowers blood sugar levels. It was developed in the 1950s in Germany.

Over the next 20 years, companies worked on ways for people with diabetes to manage their disease. In 1969, Ames Diagnostics developed the first automated glucose-measurement device people could use at home. Prior to this invention, people with diabetes had to visit their doctors to get their blood sugar levels tested. In 1973, US engineer Dean Kamen invented a wearable insulin pump that automatically delivered insulin to the bloodstream.

A major milestone for diabetes care came in 1982. Prior to that year, all insulin came from animal sources, primarily cows and pigs. These insulins worked for many people, but for some they were much less effective. In 1978, David Goeddel and his team at the drug company Genentech discovered a way to isolate and recreate human insulin in a lab. They took the human gene that is responsible for creating insulin and inserted it into bacteria cells. These cells started to produce human insulin. In 1983, Genentech and another drug company, Eli Lilly, released the first human insulin for people with diabetes to use.

Thirteen years later, researchers developed the first synthetic insulins. Lispro, a short-acting insulin, became available to people with diabetes in 1996. Four years later, researchers produced a long-acting synthetic insulin called glargine. Since then, researchers have focused on developing medications to better control blood sugar levels.

Other people have worked to improve the outcomes of those who receive pancreatic transplants. Surgeons at the University of Minnesota did the first pancreatic transplant in 1966. Since then, physicians have studied how pancreatic transplants might be

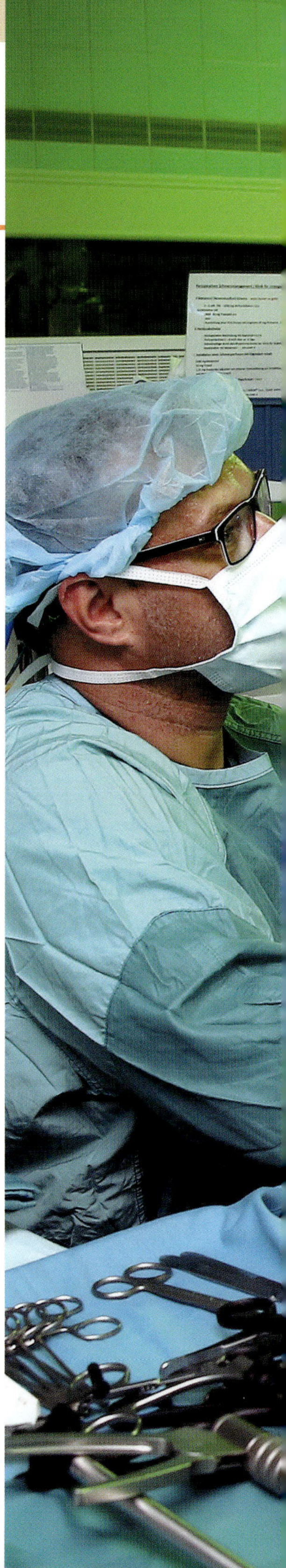

used to cure diabetes. As with other organ transplants, a major obstacle is how to prevent a person's body from rejecting the transplanted pancreas. Other researchers are studying how human genetics play a role in diabetes.

A SAD Reality

Diabetes is an ancient disease. But until relatively recently, the number of people living with the disease has been low. In 1958, 1.6 million Americans lived with diabetes. That was approximately 0.93 percent of the US population. In 2018, 34.2 million Americans lived with the disease. This was approximately 10.5 percent of the US population.[7] The Centers for Disease Control and Prevention (CDC) estimates another 84.1 million Americans have prediabetes.[8] If untreated, people with prediabetes will develop type 2 diabetes.

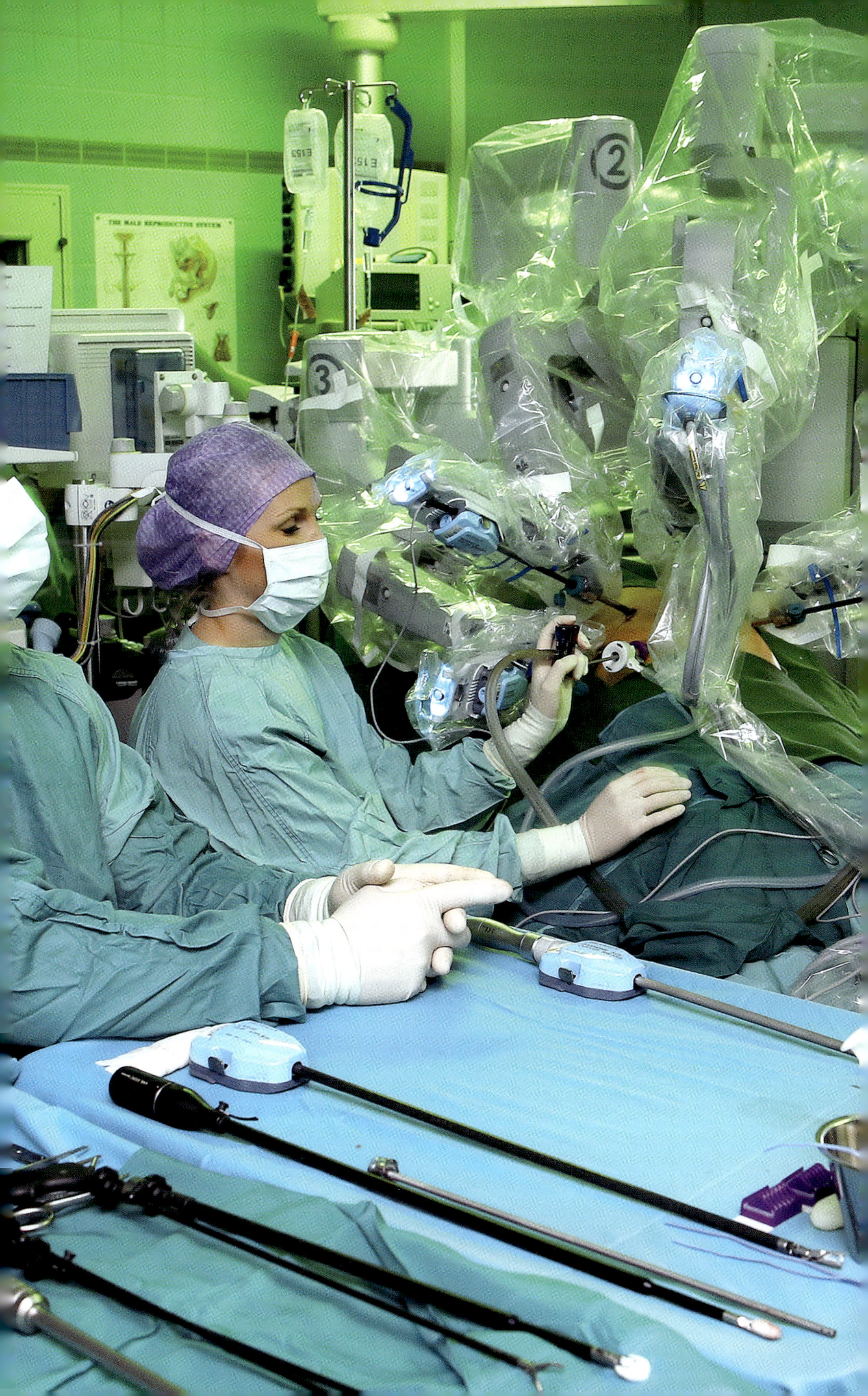

Public health experts believe the dramatic rise in cases of diabetes is related to the rise in obesity in the United States. Being overweight or obese is a risk factor for developing diabetes. In 1990, less than 15 percent of the adults in the United States were obese.[9] By 2017, that number had grown to 42.4 percent.[10]

One of the factors that is causing this rise in obesity is what is called the Standard American Diet (SAD). Only 25 percent of the US population eats the recommended amount of vegetables, fruits, and dairy foods. Meanwhile, more than half of Americans eat more grains and protein than they need.[11] Most Americans eat more sodium, sugar, and saturated fat than the body requires. Foods high in carbohydrates, sodium, sugar, and saturated fat are more caloric than whole grains, lean proteins, fruits, and vegetables. When someone eats more calories than the body needs, the body stores the extra energy as fat. This, along with genetic factors, is what causes someone to become overweight or obese.

While diabetes has been affecting people for thousands of years, it has become much more common in the last three decades. Researchers and public health experts continue to work to improve the treatment for diabetes and find a cure. They also want to keep people from developing the disease in the first place.

Diabetes and Asian Americans

Asian American adults are 40 percent more likely than white adults in the United States to be diagnosed with diabetes. Approximately 11.4 percent of Asian American adults have the disease.[13] However, experts believe the actual number may be higher. Most Asian Americans are not overweight, but that does not mean that most Asian Americans have a low risk for diabetes. Studies show that people of Asian heritage have more fat and less muscle than people in other ethnic groups. Rather than being stored under the skin, where it is visible, this extra fat is stored around the organs. This type of fat is called visceral fat. Too much visceral fat can put strain on the organs and is a risk factor for diabetes.

Chapter

Five

The Role of Nutrition

When people are diagnosed with diabetes, one of the first things addressed in their management plans is how to create and maintain a healthy diet. The foods people eat have a dramatic effect on their blood sugar levels throughout the day. It is not as simple as eating certain foods and avoiding others. People with diabetes learn to plan well-balanced meals, control their carbohydrate intake and portion sizes, and figure out how to use their insulin around meals. This is true whether they are making their meals at home or going out to eat.

Nutrition 101

Well-balanced meals include a mix of different types of foods for the body to use. These foods should contain the three key macronutrients. These are fats, proteins, and carbohydrates. The body uses fats to

Dietitians can help people with diabetes develop healthy meal plans.

Macro and Micro Nutrients

Carbohydrates, proteins, and fats are the primary macronutrients the body needs in large amounts to survive and thrive. They provide energy in the form of calories. One gram of carbohydrate or protein provides four calories. One gram of fat provides nine calories. But the body needs more than just the energy macronutrients provide. It also needs smaller amounts of vitamins and minerals to function correctly. These nutrients are called micronutrients. They include vitamin C, vitamin A, vitamin D, calcium, potassium, iron, and zinc, among many others. Most micronutrients are found in fruits, vegetables, and whole grains as well as in some dairy and other animal foods. Together, macronutrients and micronutrients round out a balanced and healthy diet.

protect vital organs and store extra energy to use later. Fats are found in nuts, seeds, oils, dairy, fish, and meat. Proteins are what the body uses to build bones, tissues, muscles, hair, skin, nails, and other parts of the body. They are an essential part of the body's hormone system too. Proteins are found in legumes, soy, nuts, seeds, whole grains, and meat. Carbohydrates provide fuel to the brain and the body. The body uses carbohydrates as easy-to-use energy sources during physical activity. But if carbohydrates are not used up, the body stores the extra energy as fats. Carbohydrates are found in grains, dairy, and fruit.

All macronutrients are important parts of

a healthy diet. But carbohydrates have the most significant effect on blood sugar levels. Eating lots of carbohydrates in one sitting may spike blood sugar to dangerously high levels. However, not eating enough carbohydrates can cause blood sugar to crash. Many people with diabetes take insulin before a meal in anticipation of blood sugar spikes. Knowing how many carbohydrates they are eating helps them dose their insulin accurately and safely.

Carbohydrate counting is the most common way for people with diabetes to manage their

carbohydrate intake. They work with their doctors to determine how many grams of carbohydrates they can safely eat in a day. To count carbohydrates, people must know which foods contain them and understand how many carbohydrates are in a serving of those foods. Then, they must determine whether they are eating a full serving, half serving, or more than one serving. Some people record their daily carbohydrates in a small notebook. Others choose to use an app on their phone.

The Diabetes Diet

The healthiest diet for someone with diabetes is the same as the healthiest diet for anyone. This is a diet that includes foods rich in nutrients and low in calories and fat. Nutrient-rich foods include fruits, vegetables, whole grains, lean proteins, and heart-healthy fats. Eating well-balanced meals timed throughout the day is an important factor in a diabetes management plan. Eating more carbohydrates and fat than the body can use causes blood sugar levels to rise. It can also cause obesity, heart disease, and high blood pressure. Planning out meals and eating a wide range of healthy foods helps many people manage their disease and prevent complications.

The best diet for people with diabetes includes healthy carbohydrates, high-fiber foods, fish, and healthy fats. It can also include lean proteins. Healthy carbohydrates, such as fruits and whole grains, include fiber. Fiber is the part of a plant that the body cannot break down. The fiber slows down how fast the body can break down carbohydrates into sugar. Eating healthy carbohydrates that are rich in fiber

Refined v. Whole Grains

Most people get their carbohydrates from grain foods. Grains include cereals, rice, bran, oatmeal, popcorn, pasta, bread, and crackers. All grain foods start as whole grains. To be whole grain, a grain seed must still have the bran and germ. All of the nutrients and fiber are still present. Many refined grains, such as white rice, white bread, and highly processed foods, have these nutrients taken out of them as they are being made. This makes refined grains less nutritious than whole grain foods. Refined grains are easily digested by the body. Eating too many may cause blood sugar levels to spike. Whole grains, on the other hand, take longer to digest. They provide energy to the body over time. Eating whole grains can help people feel full longer and control their blood sugar levels.

can help control blood sugar levels. Healthy diets are also low in sugary drinks, junk foods, fatty meats, and salty foods.

Many types of fish are excellent sources of lean protein and healthy fat. Salmon, tuna, and sardines contain omega-3 fatty acids, which are substances that protect the heart from heart disease. People with diabetes often choose to broil or bake their fish rather than fry it. Fried fish are prepared in unhealthy fats and oils. Chicken breasts and lean cuts of pork and beef are other healthy protein sources.

For healthy sources of fat, many people with diabetes eat nuts, seeds, and avocados. They might choose to cook their foods in olive oil or peanut oil. Most people living with diabetes try to cut back on high-fat dairy foods and processed snacks. These foods contain high levels of unhealthy fats that can lead to complications down the road.

A Typical Day

Planning every meal for every day can be intimidating at first. That is why some people with diabetes work with dietitians to put together meal plans. Once they have practice, it becomes easier to manage meal planning. The American Diabetes Association is a nonprofit research organization that supports people living with diabetes. It recommends a person fill half the plate at each meal with vegetables such as spinach, carrots, and tomatoes. Then, the person can fill half the remaining part of the plate with a lean protein. For the last part of the plate, a person should choose a whole grain or starchy vegetable such as a potato, adding an optional fruit for dessert.

For someone living with diabetes, a typical breakfast may be an egg white omelet

"Start off with a small portion and wait 20 minutes. Give your stomach enough time to tell your brain that you've eaten and are getting full."[2]

—Kathy McManus, director of nutrition, Brigham and Women's Hospital

with a cup of spinach, a piece of whole-grain toast with two teaspoons of jam, and a piece of fruit. For lunch, he or she might have a turkey sandwich with lettuce and tomato, a slice of cheese, an apple, and a glass of water. Popcorn is a fiber-rich food that is a good choice for a snack. For dinner, someone might broil a salmon fillet with olive oil, have a baked potato, and heat up some green beans.

Trip to the Grocery Store

Putting together a healthy meal plan is the first step toward managing diabetes through diet. The next step is to go grocery shopping. Shopping for healthy foods can be difficult at first. Nutrition and other food labels can be tricky to read. Food shopping on an empty stomach can lead people to make unhealthy choices too.

To help them make healthy choices, people living with diabetes often plan their shopping lists ahead of time. They look at the meals they plan to make for the week and purchase the ingredients they need. Some people choose to stock up on frozen vegetables and fruits so they can choose healthy options anytime. Most fresh foods, such as vegetables, meat, and dairy, are often located

Diabetes among White Americans

Approximately 7.5 percent of white American adults live with diabetes.[3] Whites are more likely to be diagnosed with type 1 diabetes than Black and Latino adults. They are also slightly more likely than people of color to develop heart disease and experience strokes as a result of their diabetes. However, as a group, white Americans have better access to health insurance and health care than people of color in the United States. As a result, they tend to experience fewer amputations due to diabetes complications, such as nerve damage and infections in the feet.

around the perimeters of grocery stores. By avoiding the aisles, people can avoid many unhealthy, highly processed foods.

Reading food labels can be a challenge for people who are counting carbohydrates and limiting calories and unhealthy fats. Most food is required to have a nutrition label. This label tells shoppers the size of a serving, how many servings are in the container, and what nutrients are in each serving. A nutrition label includes the number of calories as well as the amount of fat, cholesterol, sodium, carbohydrates, added sugars, fiber, and protein. It also shares the vitamins and minerals a food contains.

People living with diabetes try to avoid buying foods that are high in carbohydrates, fat, and added sugar and low in fiber. Often, these are junk foods such as candy, chips, crackers, and cookies. Instead, they choose foods with whole grains and low sugar contents, such as 12-grain bread and unsweetened applesauce.

Eating a healthy diet is an essential part of a diabetes management plan. Eating lots of healthy foods and cutting back on unhealthy ones can keep blood sugar levels under control. It can prevent other complications from diabetes from appearing. People who have loved ones with diabetes can support them by making healthy eating choices too.

People with diabetes should avoid going to fast-food restaurants often. Usually, the foods there have lots of fat, sugar, and salt.

Chapter
Six

Managing Diabetes

When people have diabetes, they will have to manage the disease for the rest of their life. People will need to test their blood sugar and take insulin at school and work. They will need to manage their blood sugar when they play sports, take a vacation, or get sick. Following a diabetes management plan is a long-term commitment that can affect people's relationships with their loved ones as well as their mental health.

Managing Diabetes at School

Students who live with diabetes have their parents to help them choose healthy foods and keep their blood sugar levels under control at home. But at school, they are responsible for managing their disease. Older students who have lived with diabetes for a length of time may be able to manage their diabetes completely on their own. They check their blood sugar levels,

Blood glucose meters are also known as glucometers. A person using this device puts his or her blood on a test strip.

administer insulin, and make healthy snack and lunch choices independently. Parents and students work together to make sure students have their blood sugar monitoring equipment, insulin, glucose tablets, and snacks that can increase blood sugar levels quickly. Many students wear medical bracelets to identify themselves as diabetic. This lets first responders know that the person may need glucose tablets or insulin.

Often, teachers and school nurses are able to help. With guidance from the student's doctor, teachers can look for signs of low or high blood sugar and keep juice boxes or sugar tablets in the classroom. Teachers must allow students with diabetes to have snacks if they feel their blood sugar is low. School nurses can help students monitor their blood sugar levels and administer insulin. All adults at schools should know the signs of hypoglycemia and be able to help in an emergency.

Diabetes and Sports

Physical activity is an important part of a diabetes management plan. It helps burn up energy and keeps blood sugar levels under control. Vigorous exercise, such as playing soccer, basketball, baseball, or going for a run, can cause blood sugar levels to dip. People who live with diabetes and enjoy playing sports have to consider their blood sugar while exercising.

Exercise often lowers blood sugar. So, before a game or a run, people with diabetes may eat or drink something sugary to boost their blood sugar levels. Some may turn down their insulin pumps to slow the delivery of insulin while they work out. During a game or workout, people

Healthy Snacks for School and Sports

It is important for someone with diabetes to eat at regular times. This helps keep her blood sugar levels from getting too high or too low. This might mean she needs to eat a snack during the school day or before and during sporting events. School snacks should help someone feel full without causing a big spike in blood sugar levels. Good choices include an apple, granola bar, strawberries, hummus, or a cheese stick. Athletes also need healthy snacks that will keep their blood sugar levels up while they work out. Granola bars, yogurt, fruit juice, and crackers make good choices for athletes before, during, and after workouts.

If people don't stay hydrated while they exercise, their blood sugar levels can get disrupted. People with diabetes need to drink water before, during, and after exercising.

with diabetes will drink sports drinks or take glucose tablets to ensure their blood sugar levels do not drop too low. Some people choose to bring along snacks and a backup form of insulin just in case. After their activity is over, they will eat a small snack and check their blood sugar levels. If people have a full day of exercise, it is possible for their blood sugar levels to decrease overnight. In these cases, they may need to adjust their insulin pumps to maintain safe blood sugar levels throughout the night.

Managing Diabetes at Work

Many teenagers and adults with diabetes must manage their disease at work. Like students at school, workers usually bring along snacks, insulin, and their blood sugar testing equipment to use while they are at work. Many people choose to bring their own lunches to work to ensure they are making healthy choices and eating the right amount of carbohydrates. It is a good idea for employees to tell their bosses that they live with diabetes in case a diabetic emergency occurs at work.

Employers should know and look out for the signs of hypoglycemia and provide

Protecting the Rights of Workers with Diabetes

In 2008, a change to the Americans with Disabilities Act (ADA) included people living with diabetes under the protections of that law. This means people with diabetes cannot be discriminated against at the workplace. Nor can they be denied a job or fired from a job due to their diabetes. It also requires employers to make adjustments to the workplace to accommodate a worker's diabetes, if needed. An employer may need to provide a place for someone to check his blood sugar levels or inject insulin. The employer may need to adjust work hours or duties to accommodate a worker's diabetes management plan or complications that arise from his disease. While not all workers with diabetes need these changes, some do.

space and time for people with diabetes to manage their disease. But the easiest way to know how to help employees with diabetes is to ask them. Some people will be able to manage their disease with no changes to their workplaces. But others may appreciate being able to store their snacks, insulin, and testing equipment close to their work area, or having a private place to test their blood sugar levels.

At Home and on Vacation

People spend many hours a day at school, at work, or playing sports. But they spend many more hours at home. Managing diabetes at home or while on vacation includes eating healthy meals and getting regular exercise. It also includes having medications and devices on hand to control blood sugar and insulin levels, even during emergencies. Building healthy habits at home helps prevent complications from diabetes in the long term.

Many people who live with diabetes find it helpful to have a day planner for keeping track of their management plan. People with diabetes check their blood sugar levels several times a day. Adding blood sugar levels to a calendar can show trends over time. Keeping a carbohydrate count in a planner makes it easy to see how many carbohydrates someone has eaten so far that day. Some people include their daily walks, bike rides, and other physical activity. Others choose to include when they check their feet for injuries or visit the doctor.

The need to manage diabetes does not go away when it is time for a family vacation. To prepare for vacation, people with diabetes can speak with their doctors about their travel plans and how they may affect their diabetes care. Their doctors may recommend adjusting insulin doses or extend prescriptions to cover the trip. Many people choose to get a doctor's note explaining their diabetes management plan and need for supplies. This can be helpful at the airport and with other authorities. The CDC recommends people with diabetes travel with twice as much medicine as they think they need. The organization also recommends packing insulin, glucose tablets, and healthy snacks in a cooler while traveling.

Managing diabetes while ill can be challenging. It is difficult for someone to control their blood sugar levels when they are nauseous or have a fever. Despite feeling unwell, it is important that people with diabetes continue to test their blood sugar levels and take their insulin. To prepare for when they

Going to College with Diabetes

For many young people living with diabetes, going to college is the first time they have the opportunity to manage their disease on their own. Before arriving on campus, most college students with diabetes move their prescriptions to a pharmacy close to campus. That way they have easy access to the medications they need. Most people with diabetes find it helpful to talk to their roommates and friends about their disease. Sometimes, these conversations come easily. Other times, they are more difficult. But it is important that people with diabetes feel they can rely on the people they live with to spot the signs of hypoglycemia and other complications. It also helps to talk with professors and student services about how the disease may affect coursework.

Parents can teach their children how to properly monitor their diabetes.

become sick, many people keep easy-to-eat foods on hand. These can include juice, sports drinks, soup, crackers, and unsweetened applesauce. These are foods that are easy on the body and simple to prepare. They are also less likely to cause a spike in blood sugar levels.

Friends, Family, and Mental Health

When a loved one is diagnosed with diabetes, it affects the whole family and often friends too.

Parents, partners, and adult children often help someone manage his or her disease, especially at first. It is common for people to struggle to accept their new normal, which can strain relationships with friends and family members. Loved ones want to be supportive and may not know how. The best way to maintain healthy relationships with loved ones is to be open and honest about how everyone is feeling. People living with diabetes can be clear about the type of support they would like.

Being diagnosed with an uncurable, chronic illness can cause a wide range of emotions. Someone may feel sad, scared, broken, angry, frustrated, and anxious. These emotions may change or go away with time. But often, people living with diabetes experience one or more of these emotions throughout their lives. People living with diabetes are two to three times more likely to experience depression than people without the disease.[3] If people with diabetes start to feel sad, empty, very tired, anxious, or if they are sleeping too much or too little, they may be experiencing depression. Their doctors can recommend treatment to help them feel better.

Depression, anxiety, and stress can make it difficult for someone to follow through on his or her diabetes management plan. Stress hormones can cause blood sugar levels to spike or drop. There are several things people can do to manage stress and anxiety. Taking a walk or a bike ride can help, as can doing yoga or practicing deep breathing. Talking to a friend or family member can be helpful too.

Staying Positive

No one can stay positive all the time. But trying to have a positive attitude while managing diabetes can make living with the disease easier. Talking with a friend, family member, or someone else with diabetes can be helpful. If someone is feeling unmotivated to manage his disease, it can help to set small goals to work toward. For example, someone could try to walk, run, or bike five days every week. Once he achieves this goal, he can reward himself with a bowling night, seeing a movie, or another fun activity. Finding success with smaller goals can make the big picture seem less overwhelming.

Chapter
Seven

Preventing Type 2 Diabetes

Type 1 diabetes is an autoimmune disease. It cannot be prevented. But type 2 diabetes is an acquired illness. People can avoid developing the disease. This is true even if they have a family history of type 2 diabetes or are a member of an ethnic group with a higher risk. Being at a higher risk for a disease does not mean someone will get that disease.

Building Healthy Habits

What someone eats and how much she moves every day have a big impact on her chances of developing type 2 diabetes. So does her weight. By making healthy eating choices and staying active, it is possible for a person to keep her weight in a healthy range.

Staying active can help prevent diabetes, even if someone has a family history of the disease.

These healthy habits will lower her risk of developing type 2 diabetes.

Doctors can help people learn what foods are healthy choices. Teenagers and young adults are able to make their own decisions about what they eat. By working with their doctors, they can make sure healthy choices outnumber unhealthy ones.

Even when someone knows how to make healthy choices, it can be difficult to do so all the time. Friends and family members may want to snack on junk food instead of healthy snacks, or grab a coffee drink filled with full-fat dairy and sugar. Enjoying these types of foods is OK every once in a

Building Healthy Bites

There is more to healthy eating than good food choices. How someone prepares and eats her food can make a meal healthy or unhealthy. Frying a healthy, lean protein in oil can turn a healthy choice into an unhealthy one. Broiling, baking, poaching, and sautéing are ways to cook foods without adding extra fat, sugar, or salt. When food looks and tastes great, it can be easy to eat more than the body needs. Using a smaller plate can help someone feel full faster. The smaller plate tricks her brain into feeling full. Turning off the television can help people notice how much they are eating too. People tend to eat less when the television is off. Someone who eats slowly and enjoys the taste of every bite of food tends to eat less food than someone who eats quickly without noting the taste of her food.

while. But they should not make up the majority of someone's diet.

Making healthy food choices is just one way to prevent type 2 diabetes. Being physically active most days is a healthy habit too. There are many ways to keep the body moving. Bike riding, swimming, and dancing are great options. So are playing team sports and playing a game of catch in the backyard. Hiking, canoeing, and rock climbing are all great choices too. Taking the stairs instead of the elevator or parking farther from the store can increase physical activity throughout the day. Being physically active can be more enjoyable with a friend. People who exercise with others are more likely to continue to be physically active.

Sometimes, people want to build healthier habits so they can lose weight. Being overweight or obese is a risk factor for type 2 diabetes. If someone loses just 5 to 10 percent of his body weight, he can lower his risk for developing type 2 diabetes. For someone who weighs 200 pounds (91 kg), this would mean losing 10 to 20 pounds (4.5 to 9 kg).[1] Before starting their weight loss plans, people should speak with their doctors. Doctors will make sure people lose weight in a healthy way that is tailored to their goals and lifestyles. Doctors may help patients identify healthy foods to eat. They may encourage people to pick foods that have less saturated fats, trans fats, and added sugars. Doctors may recommend eating only small portions of foods with high amounts of sugars, fats, and calories. They'll also likely tell patients to avoid high-sugar drinks, such as soda. They may want patients to eat more vegetables, fruits, and lean proteins.

People can work out from home, but they should research how to do certain exercises properly. This will help them avoid getting hurt.

Understanding Prediabetes

Often, it is possible for doctors to tell whether someone is at high risk for developing type 2 diabetes. Nearly everyone who has type 2 diabetes had prediabetes before his or her diagnosis. Someone with prediabetes usually does not have any symptoms. However, her blood sugar levels are higher than normal. The body is becoming resistant to insulin. This means the body's cells do not respond to insulin and have a more difficult time using glucose for energy. Instead, the glucose stays in the bloodstream. The body then makes more insulin to reduce blood sugar levels. But these levels are not yet high enough to be considered diabetes. In the United States, experts estimate that more than 88 million people have prediabetes.[5] If left untreated, prediabetes will develop into type 2 diabetes within five years.

To diagnose prediabetes, doctors use the same tests they use to determine whether someone has diabetes. They will administer an A1C test and a fasting blood sugar test. If the A1C test shows blood sugar levels between 5.7 and 6.4 percent, someone has prediabetes. If the fasting blood sugar test shows a fasting blood sugar level between 100 and 125 mg/dL, someone has prediabetes.

A diagnosis of prediabetes is a call to action. If someone with prediabetes loses weight, eats more healthy foods, controls portion sizes, and gets more exercise, he can lower his blood sugar levels and avoid developing type 2 diabetes.

Symptoms of Metabolic Syndrome

Metabolic syndrome is a group of conditions that someone may experience at the same time. Some of these conditions are high blood sugar and blood pressure, atypical cholesterol levels, and a lot of fat around the waist. Having metabolic syndrome puts someone at risk of developing type 2 diabetes, heart disease, and stroke. Experts believe as many as one-third of adults in the United States have metabolic syndrome.[7]

People who are overweight or obese and who are physically inactive are at risk of developing metabolic syndrome. These are also risk factors for prediabetes and type 2 diabetes. People with metabolic syndrome may also be insulin resistant.

Become a Health Champion

Making healthy choices can be difficult. Friends and family members may not wish to make similar choices. But by making healthy choices, someone can not only improve his own health but also show his loved ones how easy it is to eat healthy foods and get more exercise. Become a health champion by packing a healthy lunch and eating it at school with friends. Eat a breakfast with protein, fiber, and fruit before heading to school or work. Walk or bike to school if it is safe to do so. Get involved with a sport at school. Offer to help make the family grocery list so healthy foods get in the house.

Heart Disease and Diabetes

Heart disease is the leading cause of death in the United States. This is true for both men and women, and for people of most ethnic groups. Approximately 647,000 people die from heart disease every year.[8] Risk factors for heart disease include high blood pressure, being overweight or obese, eating an unhealthy diet, and having diabetes. Adults living with diabetes are nearly twice as likely to die from heart disease as people who do not have diabetes.[9] Having high blood sugar levels can damage blood vessels over time. High blood sugar can also harm the nerves that control the blood vessels and the heart. The longer someone has lived with diabetes, the more likely she is to develop heart disease.

Most of the time, metabolic syndrome has few symptoms. Doctors may suspect someone has metabolic syndrome if she has one or more of the risk factors.

Someone who is diagnosed with metabolic syndrome is more likely to develop type 2 diabetes. Eventually, the body's resistance to insulin becomes so severe that the pancreas cannot make enough insulin to control blood sugar levels. This leads to type 2 diabetes.

It is possible to prevent metabolic syndrome. If someone is considered at risk of developing the condition, he can work with his doctor to develop a weight loss plan. This should include healthy food choices, portion control, and at least 30 minutes of exercise most days. These lifestyle changes can prevent metabolic syndrome from developing.

Type 2 diabetes is a preventable disease, even if someone is at higher risk of developing it. Building healthy eating habits, moving more, and maintaining a healthy weight can prevent type 2 diabetes. These things can also prevent prediabetes and metabolic syndrome, which can lead to type 2 diabetes.

Chapter *Eight*

Ongoing Research

Diabetes affects one in eight Americans.[1] But funding for diabetes research is much lower than for certain other diseases. This means treatments and potential cures for diabetes may be delayed or not discovered at all.

The American Diabetes Association works to increase funding for diabetes research. Part of the organization's research efforts is the Pathway to Stop Diabetes. This program provides funding for researchers studying diabetes, especially for younger researchers who are new to the field. The American Diabetes Association hopes its funding will help creative researchers uncover new insights about diabetes prevention and treatment.

In 2019, a group of kids with type 1 diabetes went to a US Senate meeting that discussed the disease.

Understanding Diabetes

Several projects funded by the Pathway to Stop Diabetes program have improved doctors' understanding of diabetes. The program also has funded studies into what may cause someone to develop diabetes. One 2019 study may have found one of the causes of type 1 diabetes. The study was intended to work on a new immunotherapy treatment for type 1 diabetes. Most treatments for autoimmune diseases treat the entire immune system. The study looked at ways to address just the part of the immune

The SEARCH Study

The SEARCH for Diabetes in Youth study is a long-term research project. Researchers want to understand how diabetes affects US children and young adults. The study started in 2000 and continued through 2020. More than 27,000 people in ten states participated.[2] The study has revealed a lot about how diabetes affects children. Between 2001 and 2009, rates of both types of diabetes rose for children of most ages, genders, and ethnic groups. Children with diabetes are more likely to be overweight or obese. The study found that many children ate few fruits and vegetables and did not get enough exercise. Many adolescents with diabetes have trouble controlling their blood sugar levels as they make the transition from childhood to adulthood. Some children with diabetes developed complications. These included early-stage kidney disease and nerve damage.

system that targets beta cells in the pancreas. It focused on one molecule called immunoglobulin M (IgM). The researchers found the IgM molecule can cause the immune system to stop attacking beta cells. The study found the IgM molecules in people with type 1 diabetes do not stop the immune system. More research is needed. But if people with type 1 diabetes can receive IgM cells from people without the disease, they may be able to reverse their diabetes.

Another 2019 study looked at how a synthetic chemical affected the risk someone had of developing diabetes. Bisphenol A (BPA) is used to make certain plastics, such as plastic water bottles and the lining of aluminum cans. The study looked at the effect BPA had on blood sugar levels. It found that BPA had an immediate, direct effect. The researchers planned to expand the study to look at BPA's effects on blood sugar over a long period of time.

Other studies researched how diabetes affects younger and older populations. One 2019 study looked at the brains and hormonal systems of children with obesity. Together, the brain and the hormonal system regulate how and when people feel full after a meal. The study found the hormonal systems of children with obesity send signals of feeling full just as the systems of healthy-weight children do. But the brains of children with obesity do not respond as well. This may be why many children with obesity struggle to feel full and lose weight.

Another 2019 study wanted to answer why older people tend to be more at risk for developing diabetes. The study looked at the beta cells in the pancreases of mice. It found that the mice had a combination of older beta cells and younger beta cells. Some of the cells were as old as the mice themselves, while others were more recently created. Researchers believe the younger cells work

How the Body Feels Full

Feeling full is the body's way of knowing it has eaten enough food. When someone eats, her stomach fills up and her blood sugar rises. The body's temperature also rises. Fat cells help the body feel full and regulate its weight. Fat cells release a hormone called leptin. Leptin travels to a region of the brain called the hypothalamus. When leptin levels are low, the hypothalamus triggers hunger in the body. When leptin levels are high, it signals the body to stop eating.

better than the older ones do. They hoped to expand the study to look at how to increase the creation of younger beta cells in older adults.

Innovations in Diabetes Medicines

Some research focuses on understanding the causes of diabetes. Other studies look into new medicines and technologies to treat diabetes or even find a cure. One of these studies found a new molecule that could be helpful for monitoring blood sugar. Many people with diabetes use continuous blood glucose monitoring devices. These devices keep track of an enzyme's activity to make their calculations. But the activity can change over time, which means someone's monitor may produce inaccurate blood sugar readings. Researchers have developed a brand-new molecule that can be used within continuous glucose monitors. This molecule does not rely on an enzyme to produce blood sugar readings. This could make continuous glucose monitors more accurate.

Another study looked at a different type of molecule called ceramide. The study found the ceramide molecule is responsible for causing mice cells to become insulin resistant. The researchers

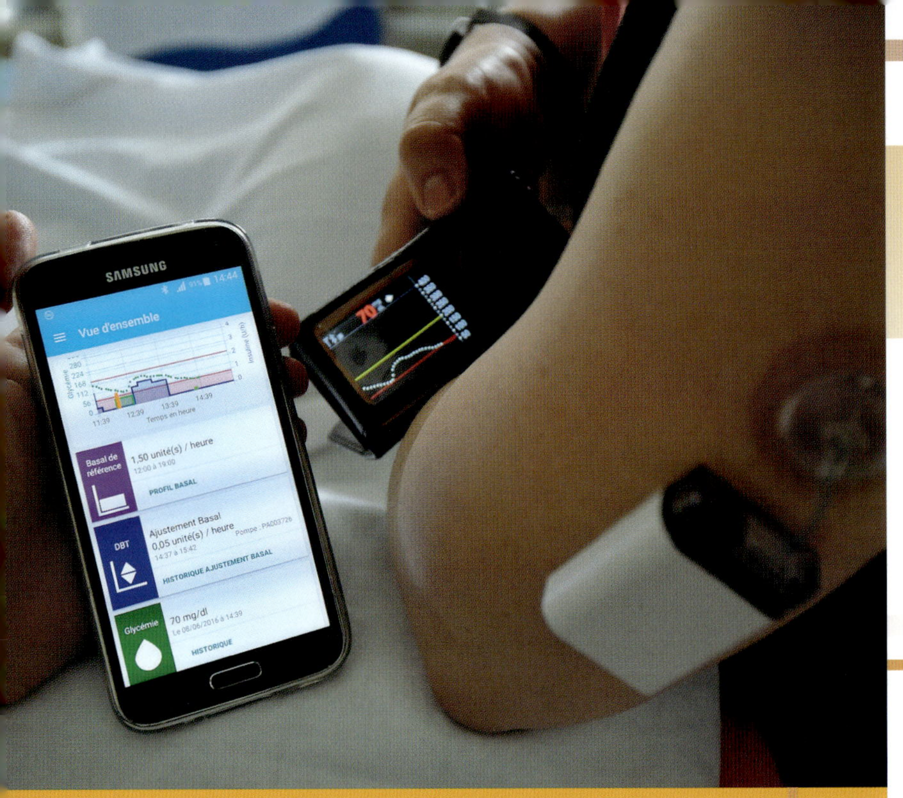

An individual with an artificial pancreas tested out a smartphone app in France. The app helps people monitor their insulin levels.

want to expand their study to look at how ceramide molecules work in humans. Their work may find a way to reduce ceramide molecules in people with type 2 diabetes.

Innovations in Diabetes Technologies

Many people with type 1 diabetes rely on technologies that automatically monitor their blood sugar levels and deliver insulin. Such a system is known as an artificial pancreas. An artificial pancreas system was approved by the Food and Drug Administration in 2016. The system can adjust short-acting insulin levels automatically based on blood sugar levels. However, wearers still need to count carbohydrates and enter them into their monitor. They also need to manually administer insulin during blood sugar spikes.

Since then, several other hybrid artificial pancreas systems have also become available to people with type 1 diabetes. Most can automatically shut off the insulin pump when blood sugar levels drop below a certain number. Others can predict when blood sugar levels will drop and automatically reduce insulin levels. More advanced systems can adjust the release of short-acting insulin if blood sugar levels drop or rise.

These systems are not fully automated. But fully automated artificial pancreas systems will eventually be available. In 2020, systems that deliver fast-acting insulin to bring down high blood sugar levels became available. People anticipated that several years after that, systems would also be able to detect when wearers eat meals and automatically dose fast-acting insulin. Wearers will not have to enter carbohydrate counts or give themselves insulin in addition to what their systems provide.

The Juvenile Diabetes Research Foundation (JDRF) is a global organization that funds research for type 1 diabetes. The organization hopes to improve the lives of people with type 1 diabetes and eventually create a world where the disease no longer exists. One of the initiatives JDRF supports is universal screening for type 1 diabetes. Type 1 diabetes is a disease that can affect anyone. Presently, people need to suffer symptoms of type 1 diabetes before they are diagnosed. If symptoms are severe, such as diabetic ketoacidosis, this can put someone's life in danger.

Screening could indicate whether people have type 1 diabetes before they show symptoms. Universal screening would make screening available to every child. In 2019, JDRF funded a study of 90,632 German children ages two to five.[4] The purpose of the study was to see whether universal screening could catch more cases before children experienced diabetic ketoacidosis. The group hoped this would provide evidence that the benefits of universal screening outweighed the costs. Of the 90,632 children screened, 280 had type 1 diabetes but presented no symptoms. Just two of the children experienced diabetic ketoacidosis. This was a rate of less than 1 percent. In Germany, 20 percent of children with undiagnosed type 1 diabetes experience the life-threatening condition. In the United States, that figure is 40 to 60 percent.[5] JDRF says the study showed that the cost of screening every child is less than the cost of treating children for diabetic ketoacidosis. The group hopes universal screening becomes available for children around the world.

National Diabetes Prevention Program

In 2010, the CDC created the National Diabetes Prevention Program. The program, also called the National DPP, encourages people to adopt healthy habits. The goal is to reduce the number of Americans who develop type 2 diabetes. The CDC works with state and local health departments, employers, insurance companies, and community groups to implement the program.

The National DPP provides its partner organizations with topics and materials for a course that helps people build healthy habits and lose weight. It requires its partners to train lifestyle coaches to teach the program. The CDC gets reports about the progress of the people taking the program. People learn how to reduce the number of calories they eat and commit to being active at least 150 minutes a week.

Ten years after the program started, the DPP Outcomes Study looked at how well the program worked. The study found people who participated in the program were 30 percent less likely to develop type 2 diabetes.[6] Some participants did develop type 2 diabetes. But they did so four years later than they would have had they not completed the program. The study showed that making healthy choices and maintaining a healthy weight can help prevent type 2 diabetes.

"Today, nearly one in eight American adults has diabetes, and diagnosed diabetes costs the United States $245 billion each year."[7]

—*American Diabetes Association*

All of these innovations will make living with diabetes more manageable. Some may prevent people from developing the disease in the first place. For the millions of people with diabetes in the United States, this is encouraging news. Diabetes is not curable today, but with the hard work of researchers and the people who participate in their studies, a cure may be possible in the future.

Essential *Facts*

Facts about Diabetes

- Diabetes is an incurable, chronic disease that affects approximately 34.2 million Americans. More than 210,000 of these people are children.

- Type 1 diabetes is an autoimmune disease. The immune system attacks beta cells in the pancreas. There is no cure, but type 1 diabetes can be managed with insulin and diet.

- Type 2 diabetes is a disease where the pancreas gradually does not produce enough insulin or insulin is not used properly by the body. There is no cure, but type 2 diabetes can be managed by diet, exercise, and medications.

- Ten percent of Americans with diabetes have type 1 diabetes. All others have type 2 diabetes.

- Due to genetic, environmental, and social factors, people of color are more likely to develop type 2 diabetes than white people. Native Americans are more likely to develop type 2 diabetes than any other ethnic group in the United States.

- Research may uncover new treatments for people with diabetes and may eventually discover a cure.

How Diabetes Affects Daily Life

- People living with diabetes manage their disease by monitoring the carbohydrates they eat, measuring their blood sugar levels, and administering insulin injections.

- The diabetes diet includes healthy carbohydrates, high-fiber foods, fish, and healthy fats. It is low in sugary drinks, junk food, fatty meats, and salty foods.

- People with diabetes must take time out of their school or work day to monitor their blood sugar levels and inject insulin as needed.
- Some people choose to use continuous blood glucose monitors and insulin pumps to automatically track blood sugar levels and administer short-acting insulin.

How Diabetes Can Be Managed

- People living with diabetes manage their disease with a healthy diet, exercise, insulin, and the support of family and friends.
- Eating a healthy diet, exercising regularly, and maintaining a healthy weight can help someone prevent type 2 diabetes. Reversing prediabetes and metabolic syndrome can also prevent type 2 diabetes.
- In the future, artificial pancreases may completely manage a person's diabetes.

Quote

"Diabetes sounds like you're going to die when you hear it. I was immediately frightened. But once I got a better idea of what it was and that it was something I could manage myself, I was comforted."

—Nick Jonas, a singer with type 1 diabetes

Glossary

amputation

The action of surgically cutting off a limb.

autoantibody

A substance the body makes in response to a perceived threat; the substance targets the body itself.

blood vessel

A tube through which blood and some other bodily substances flow.

calorie

A unit to measure how much energy or heat a food or drink can produce when consumed.

chronic

Continuing for a long time.

dietitian

An expert in applying nutrition science to diet.

enzyme

A protein that helps break down other chemicals in the body.

gene

A unit of hereditary information found in a chromosome.

gestational diabetes

A type of diabetes that is diagnosed for the first time during pregnancy.

glycogen

A sugar molecule that is stored in muscle or liver tissue.

hormone

A regulatory substance that sparks an action, such as growth, digestion, or sexual maturation, in a tissue or organ.

immunotherapy

Treatment for a disease that involves stimulating or suppressing the body's immune system.

metabolize

To change by metabolism, the physical and chemical means by which an organism processes energy.

obesity

A medical condition where the body accumulates and stores excess fat.

screening

Testing to see whether a person has a disease.

viral

Related to or caused by a tiny parasite.

Additional Resources

Selected Bibliography

"Choose More Than 50 Ways to Prevent Type 2 Diabetes." *National Institute of Diabetes and Digestive and Kidney Diseases*, n.d., niddk.nih.gov. Accessed 15 June 2020.

"Diabetes: Symptoms & Causes." *Mayo Clinic*, n.d., mayoclinic.org. Accessed 15 June 2020.

"Newly Diagnosed." *American Diabetes Association*, n.d., diabetes.org. Accessed 15 June 2020.

Further Readings

McAllister, Patrick. *Highs & Lows of Type 1 Diabetes*. Skyhorse, 2018.

Wheeler, Jill C. *Handling Obesity*. Abdo, 2022.

Online Resources

To learn more about handling diabetes, please visit **abdobooklinks.com** or scan this QR code. These links are routinely monitored and updated to provide the most current information available.

More Information

For more information on this subject, contact or visit the following organizations:

American Diabetes Association

2451 Crystal Dr. #900
Arlington, VA 22202
800-342-2383
diabetes.org
The American Diabetes Association is an organization that supports diabetes research and provides information for people living with diabetes and their loved ones.

Centers for Disease Control and Prevention

1600 Clifton Rd.
Atlanta, GA 30329
800-232-4636
cdc.gov
The Centers for Disease Control and Prevention is the health protection agency of the United States. It protects Americans from health and safety threats.

Mayo Clinic

200 First St. SW
Rochester, MN 55905
507-284-2511
mayoclinic.org
The Mayo Clinic is one of the top hospitals in the United States. It is a trusted leader in health care for adults and children.

Source *Notes*

CHAPTER 1. LIVING WITH DIABETES

1. Amanda Griswold. "Tackling Sports and Exercise with T1D." *Medtronic*, 1 June 2017, medtronicdiabetes.com. Accessed 3 Aug. 2020.

2. "National Diabetes Statistics Report 2020." *CDC*, 2020, cdc.gov. Accessed 3 Aug. 2020.

3. "Managing Diabetes Is an Uphill Climb." *American Diabetes Association*, n.d., diabetes.org. Accessed 3 Aug. 2020.

4. "Statistics about Diabetes." *American Diabetes Association*, n.d., diabetes.org. Accessed 3 Aug. 2020.

5. "Native Americans with Diabetes." *CDC*, 10 Jan. 2017, cdc.gov. Accessed 3 Aug. 2020.

CHAPTER 2. TYPE 1 DIABETES

1. "Diabetes Mellitus: An Overview." *Cleveland Clinic*, 2 Oct. 2018, my.clevelandclinic.org. Accessed 3 Aug. 2020.

2. "Type 1 Diabetes." *CDC*, 11 Mar. 2020, cdc.gov. Accessed 3 Aug. 2020.

3. "8 Eye-Opening Quotes from Famous People with Diabetes." *No Cost Shoes*, n.d., nocostshoes.com. Accessed 3 Aug. 2020.

4. Mayo Clinic Staff. "Diabetes." *Mayo Clinic*, 8 Aug. 2018, mayoclinic.org. Accessed 3 Aug. 2020.

CHAPTER 3. TYPE 2 DIABETES

1. "Diabetes Mellitus: An Overview." *Cleveland Clinic*, 2 Oct. 2018, my.clevelandclinic.org. Accessed 3 Aug. 2020.

2. Mayo Clinic Staff. "Type 2 Diabetes in Children." *Mayo Clinic*, 31 Jan. 2020, mayoclinic.org. Accessed 3 Aug. 2020.

3. "Rates of Newly Diagnosed Cases of Type 1 and Type 2 Diabetes Continue to Rise among Children, Teens." *CDC*, 11 Feb. 2020, cdc.gov. Accessed 3 Aug. 2020.

4. "Diabetes and African Americans." *US Department of Health & Human Services*, 19 Dec. 2019, minorityhealth.hhs.gov. Accessed 3 Aug. 2020.

5. Mayo Clinic Staff. "Diabetes." *Mayo Clinic*, 8 Aug. 2018, mayoclinic.org. Accessed 3 Aug. 2020.

6. "About Prediabetes & Type 2 Diabetes." *CDC*, 4 Apr. 2019, cdc.gov. Accessed 3 Aug. 2020.

7. Mila Ferrer. "Understanding Diversity in the Hispanic Community." *Association of Diabetes Care & Education Specialists*, 5 Oct. 2017, diabeteseducator.org. Accessed 3 Aug. 2020.

8. "Life Doesn't End with Type 2 Diabetes." *American Diabetes Association*, n.d., diabetes.org. Accessed 3 Aug. 2020.

CHAPTER 4. AN ANCIENT DISEASE

1. Ananya Mandal. "History of Diabetes." *News Medical Life Sciences*, 4 June 2019, news-medical.net. Accessed 3 Aug. 2020.

2. Kenneth F. Kiple, ed. *The Cambridge World History of Food*. Cambridge UP, 2000. 1079.

3. Lee J. Sanders. "From Thebes to Toronto and the 21st Century: An Incredible Journey." *American Diabetes Association*, Jan. 2002, spectrum.diabetesjournals.org. Accessed 3 Aug. 2020.

4. Sanders, "From Thebes to Toronto and the 21st Century."

5. "The Pancreas and Its Functions." *Columbia University Irving Medical Center*, n.d., columbiasurgery.org. Accessed 3 Aug. 2020.

6. Erika Gebel. "Making Insulin." *Diabetes Forecast*, July 2013, diabetesforecast.org. Accessed 3 Aug. 2020.

7. "Long-Term Trends in Diabetes." *CDC*, Apr. 2017, cdc.gov. Accessed 3 Aug. 2020.

8. "New CDC Report: More than 100 Million Americans Have Diabetes or Prediabetes." *CDC*, 18 July 2017, cdc.gov. Accessed 3 Aug. 2020.

9. "An Epidemic of Obesity: US Obesity Trends." *Harvard School of Public Health*, n.d., hsph.harvard.edu. Accessed 3 Aug. 2020.

10. "Adult Obesity Facts." *CDC*, 29 June 2020, cdc.gov. Accessed 3 Aug. 2020.

Source Notes
Continued

11. "Shifts Needed to Align with Healthy Eating Patterns." *US Department of Health & Human Services*, n.d., health.gov. Accessed 3 Aug. 2020.

12. Ambika Satija et al. "Plant-Based Dietary Patterns and Incidence of Type 2 Diabetes in US Men and Women: Results from Three Prospective Cohort Studies." *PLOS Medicine*, 14 June 2016, journals.plos.org. Accessed 3 Aug. 2020.

13. "Diabetes and Asian Americans." *US Department of Health & Human Services*, 19 Dec. 2019, health.gov. Accessed 3 Aug. 2020.

CHAPTER 5. THE ROLE OF NUTRITION

1. Mayo Clinic Staff. "Diabetes Diet: Create Your Healthy Eating Plan." *Mayo Clinic*, 19 Feb. 2019, mayoclinic.org. Accessed 3 Aug. 2020.

2. "The Diabetic Diet." *American Heart Association*, 31 Aug. 2015, heart.org. Accessed 3 Aug. 2020.

3. "Statistics about Diabetes." *American Diabetes Association*, 2020, diabetes.org. Accessed 3 Aug. 2020.

CHAPTER 6. MANAGING DIABETES

1. "Prevent Complications." *CDC*, 1 Aug. 2019, cdc.gov. Accessed 3 Aug. 2020.

2. "Diabetes and Mental Health." *CDC*, 6 Aug. 2018, cdc.gov. Accessed 3 Aug. 2020.

3. "Diabetes and Mental Health."

CHAPTER 7. PREVENTING TYPE 2 DIABETES

1. "Your Game Plan to Prevent Type 2 Diabetes." *NIH*, Feb. 2017, niddk.nih.gov. Accessed 3 Aug. 2020.

2. "Choose More than 50 Ways to Prevent Type 2 Diabetes." *NIH*, Sept. 2014, niddk.nih.gov. Accessed 3 Aug. 2020.

3. "Global Recommendations on Physical Activity for Health." *WHO*, 2011, who.int. Accessed 3 Aug. 2020.

4. "Physical Activity and Adults." *WHO*, n.d., who.int. Accessed 3 Aug. 2020.

5. "About Prediabetes & Type 2 Diabetes." *CDC*, 4 Apr. 2019, cdc.gov. Accessed 3 Aug. 2020.

6. "About Prediabetes & Type 2 Diabetes."

7. Mayo Clinic Staff. "Metabolic Syndrome." *Mayo Clinic*, 14 Mar. 2019, mayoclinic.org. Accessed 3 Aug. 2020.

8. "Heart Disease Facts." *CDC*, 22 June 2020, cdc.gov. Accessed 3 Aug. 2020.

9. "Diabetes, Heart Disease, and Stroke." *NIH*, Feb. 2017, niddk.nih.gov. Accessed 3 Aug. 2020.

CHAPTER 8. ONGOING RESEARCH

1. "The Problem Is Unprecedented. The Solution Must Match It." *American Diabetes Association*, n.d., diabetes.org. Accessed 3 Aug. 2020.

2. "What Is the SEARCH Study?" *SEARCH for Diabetes in Youth*, n.d., searchfordiabetes.org. Accessed 3 Aug. 2020.

3. Richard F. Hamman et al. "The SEARCH for Diabetes in Youth Study: Rationale, Findings and Future Directions." *American Diabetes Association*, Dec. 2014, diabetesjournals.org. Accessed 3 Aug. 2020.

4. Alexandra Mulvey. "Universal Screening for Type 1 Diabetes: Its Time Has Come?" *JDRF*, 28 Jan. 2020, jdrf.org. Accessed 3 Aug. 2020.

5. Mulvey, "Universal Screening for Type 1 Diabetes."

6. "Research behind the National DPP." *CDC*, 4 Apr. 2019, cdc.gov. Accessed 3 Aug. 2020.

7. "The Problem Is Unprecedented. The Solution Must Match It."

Index

About the Author

A. R. Carser

A. R. Carser is a freelance writer who lives in Minnesota. She enjoys learning and writing about innovations in science and health care.

About the Consultant

Dr. Kyle Burghardt

Dr. Kyle Burghardt is an associate professor of pharmacy practice at the Eugene Applebaum College of Pharmacy and Health Sciences at Wayne State University. He teaches and conducts research in the pharmacy areas of genetics, diabetes, and mental health.